Cinderella

Cinderella lived with two mean stepsisters who made her do all the housework.

Cinderella wished she could go to a fancy ball at the Prince's palace. Magically, a kind fairy appeared and granted her wish! Cinderella's raggedy clothes turned into a beautiful blue dress and glass slippers.

The fairy warned Cinderella as her carriage rode away: "Remember, your wish ends at midnight, today!"

When the Prince danced with Cinderella he fell in love. But Cinderella knew she had to run away by midnight.

As she ran, she lost one of her glass slippers. The Prince found it, and he began to search his entire kingdom to find her.

Тhe Prince finally found Cinderella, and placed the lost slipper on her foot.

She was so happy and the Prince yelled "Hooray!" So the two of them got married the very next day!

SNOW WHITE

Snow White was the prettiest girl in the kingdom! But a jealous queen wanted to put her in jail to hide her beauty.

So she ran to the forest home of seven little dwarfs.

"You're welcome to hide here at our house!" they all exclaimed.

But the ugly queen found her! She dressed up like an old beggar woman and gave Snow White an enchanted apple.

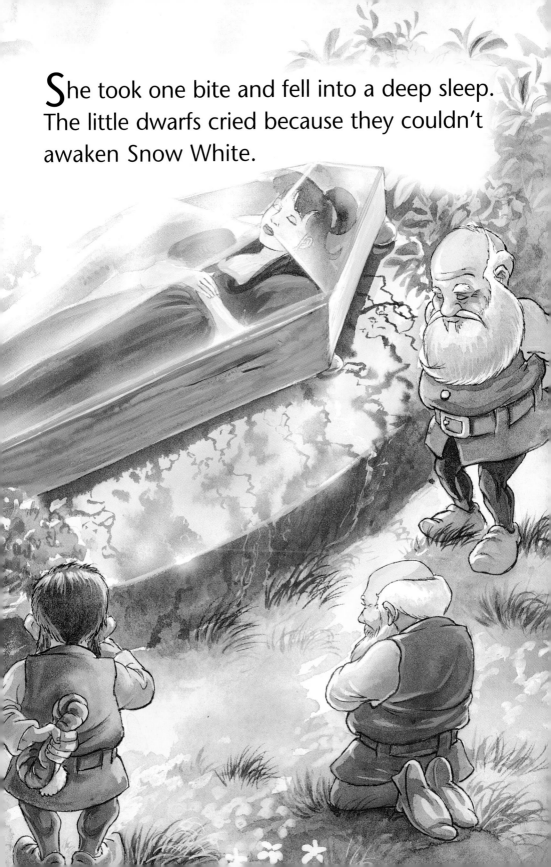

She took one bite and fell into a deep sleep. The little dwarfs cried because they couldn't awaken Snow White.

So the dwarfs put her in a glass case and prayed for help. One day, their prayers were answered when a handsome prince came by and awakened Snow White with a magic kiss.

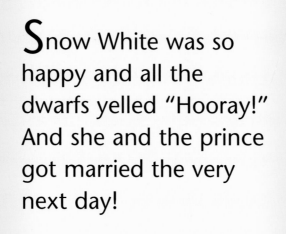

Snow White was so happy and all the dwarfs yelled "Hooray!" And she and the prince got married the very next day!